Mr FAWKES, THE KING AND THE GUNPOWDER PLOT

Published in paperback in 2017 by Wayland
Copyright © Hodder and Stoughton 2017

Wayland
Carmelite House
50 Victoria Embankment
London
EC4Y 0DZ

Wayland Australia
Level 17/207 Kent Street
Sydney NSW 2000

Editor: Katie Woolley
Cover designer: Lisa Peacock
Inside designer: Alyssa Peacock

ISBN: 978 1 5263 0346 2

Printed in China

MIX
Paper from
responsible sources
FSC   FSC® C104740
www.fsc.org

10 9 8 7 6 5 4 3 2 1

Wayland is a division of
Hachette Children's Group,
an Hachette UK company.
www.hachette.co.uk

MR FAWKES, THE KING AND THE GUNPOWDER PLOT

by Tom and Tony Bradman

Illustrated by Carlo Molinari

WAYLAND

CHARACTERS iN THiS STORY...

JACK LAMBERT
- a young boy, assistant
to Sir Robert

SIR ROBERT CECIL
- England's top spy

KING JAMES I
- the King of England

ROBERT CATESBY

THOMAS WINTOUR

JOHN WRIGHT

THOMAS PERCY

ROBERT KEYES
- plotters against the king

GUY FAWKES

**BARON
MONTEAGLE**

**THE DUKE
OF SUFFOLK**
- supporters of the king

MRS ASHBY
- a landlady

PROLOGUE

It is 1605. The Protestant King James I has been on the throne for two years, but he has enemies among England's Catholics. Soon, he is due to attend an important event in Parliament — this will provide the perfect opportunity for anyone who wants to kill him. England's top spy Sir Robert Cecil and his young helper, Jack, have heard a worrying rumour...

They have foiled plots before — but can they foil this one?

CHAPTER ONE

King James was sitting at his desk in the Palace of Whitehall. He was frowning and tugging at his beard as he read a report. Suddenly, there was a knock at the door. The king was startled and almost leapt out of his seat.

"Er… who's there?" he called out nervously. "Is that you, Sir Robert?"

The door opened and a man came in. He was tall and smartly dressed, and had piercing dark eyes. A young boy followed him.

"Yes, Your Majesty," said Sir Robert. "And this is my assistant, Jack Lambert."

Sir Robert bowed, and nudged Jack to do the same. Jack tried not to stare at the king — he had never been this close to anyone royal before.

"I see you're reading my most recent report, sire," said Sir Robert.

"Actually, I wish I wasn't," said the king. "I didn't realise so many of my subjects hated me."

"As far as we know you're very popular with, er… some of the people," said Sir Robert, smiling.

"But your report is a long list of plots against me!" groaned the king.

"True," said Sir Robert. "However, things have changed in the last few weeks. Please tell the king what the current situation is, Jack."

"There were half a dozen plots in the report, Your Majesty," said Jack. "Since then, we've uncovered even more..."

"MORE? That's terrible!" said the king, the blood draining from his face. "Why, it sounds as if things are out of control!"

"On the contrary, Your Majesty" said Sir Robert. 'In fact, we have everything *under* control. We have caught the plotters."

"But, sir," Jack whispered to his master. "We haven't caught them *all*..."

"Not now, Jack," Sir Robert hissed from the corner of his mouth. "Don't worry, sire, the entire nation will love you... eventually."

"I'll be happy if they simply don't try to kill me," the king muttered. "By the way, is everything ready for the State Opening of Parliament?"

"Very nearly, Your Majesty," said Sir Robert. "We still have a few minor security checks to make, but they shouldn't take too long."

"Well then, don't let me keep you," said the king, dismissing them.

"Of course, Your Majesty," said Sir Robert, and they left. Jack scampered after his master along the corridors of the palace.

"Sir, I don't understand," he said. 'Why didn't you tell the king about the other plot?"

"I don't want to worry him until we know more," said Sir Robert. "Hurry up now, Jack – the nation's future is in our hands!"

CHAPTER TWO

A few streets away, four men sat together round a table in the darkest corner of a seedy tavern. They each had a mug of ale but they weren't drinking much. Instead, they leaned towards each other and talked in hushed voices. The tavern was crowded, and every so often they looked over their shoulders to make sure nobody was listening to their conversation.

"So, we are agreed," said the man who was the leader of the group. His name was Robert Catesby. "King James I must die."

"Everyone who supports him must die, too," said Thomas Wintour. "His family and friends will be in Parliament that day."

"We'll need to find someone to do the job," whispered John Wright. "After all, none of us have any experience of this kind of thing."

"We're in luck," said Thomas Percy. "I've found

two men who might be able to help. I've asked them to meet us. Ah, here they are now."

Percy waved at two men who had just come into the tavern. Both of them were tall and tough-looking. They saw Percy and made their way over to the table, bringing their mugs of ale. Percy made the introductions – the two newcomers were called Guy Fawkes and Robert Keyes.

"So, gentlemen," said Wintour after a while. "Tell us about yourselves."

"There's not much to tell," said Fawkes. He shrugged and spat on the floor. "We're soldiers of fortune, Keyes and me, and we've been fighting for the Spanish king against the Protestant rebels in the Netherlands."

"Is that so? I take it you don't like the Protestants?" asked Catesby, glancing at his companions. Spain was a powerful Catholic country. The Netherlands was ruled by Spain, but many people there were Protestants.

"We don't like 'em at all," growled Keyes. He spat, too.

"So, what do you want from us?" asked Fawkes.

"We have a plan to make England a better place, but we need some help," said Catesby.

"I'm in," said Fawkes, without thinking.

Keyes nodded, too. "What's the plan?"

"Something spectacular," said Catesby. "Have you ever used gunpowder before?"

"We've blown up loads of stuff!" said Fawkes, grinning happily.

The six men shook hands, their faces firm, as they raised their mugs and drank them dry, before banging them down on the table.

"Death to King James I!" they whispered.

The next day, the men set about getting organised…

CHAPTER THREE

The first thing Catesby did was to rent a house close to the parliament building. Catesby used a street map to explain his plan to the other plotters.

"It's simple," he said. "All we have to do is dig a tunnel that goes beneath Parliament. Then, we fill it with barrels of gunpowder and BOOM!"

"I'm not doing any digging," muttered Keyes. He sat back in his seat and folded his arms, scowling at Catesby. "I'm a soldier, not a mole."

"It's not going to work, anyway," said Fawkes. "Digging a tunnel could take months, and how do we know which direction to dig in?"

"Fawkes is right," said Percy. "And what if somebody hears us digging?"

"I'm worried about something else, too," said Wintour. "A lot of innocent people might be killed if we blow up the whole building."

"Wintour has a point," said Wright. "We must be careful about how much gunpowder we use. We don't want to blow up half of London."

"It's a bit late to start worrying about all that," said Percy crossly.

Wright snapped back at him just as crossly, and soon an argument had begun. The plotters yelled at each other until a knock on the door silenced everyone.

"Er… who's there?" Catesby called out, his voice squeaky with fear.

"It's only me, your landlady, Mrs Ashby!" came the cheerful reply. "I just wanted to make sure that you gentlemen had settled in properly."

The plotters breathed out in relief. Catesby quickly folded up the map and put it away, then nodded to Percy. He opened the door and let Mrs Ashby in. She was a small lady, mostly dressed in black, but with a happy face.

"We're very pleased with the house, Mrs Ashby, thank you," said Catesby, smiling at her. "Now if that's all you wanted…"

"There was something else I wanted to tell you," she said. "I realised I'd forgotten to mention the cellar."

"What cellar, Mrs Ashby?" asked Catesby.

"The one under the house, of course!" she said.

"Interesting. And does it join up with any other cellars? We're quite close to Parliament after all," said Percy.

"Of course," said Mrs Ashby. "Only a narrow brick wall separates my cellar from theirs. Would you like to have a look round?"

"Most definitely, Mrs Ashby!" said Catesby, as four of the plotters followed her out the door. Wintour held Wright back.

"I can't let innocent people die," he whispered.

"I agree. But what can we do?" asked Wright.

"Don't worry, I have an idea," said Wintour.

CHAPTER FOUR

"Be sure to stay sharp, men," said Sir Robert. He was talking to the soldiers who were guarding the main entrance of Parliament. "I need you to be more alert than ever today. Keep your eyes peeled and your ears open."

Jack was standing beside Sir Robert. It was November 5th, the day of the Opening of

Parliament, and a crowd of people had lined up to enter – lords, ladies, archbishops and MPs, all of them finely dressed. The king and queen were due to arrive soon with their children.

"I've checked on the other guards," said Jack. "They're all in place."

"Good boy," said Sir Robert. Jack could see that he looked worried. "I only hope we've done enough. Now, what do these two want with me?"

Jack had also noticed the two lords, Baron Monteagle and the Duke of Suffolk, heading towards them.

"Ah, there you are, Sir Robert," drawled the Duke of Suffolk. "Monteagle and I have been searching for you absolutely everywhere."

"Well, you've found me," said Sir Robert. His eyes were drawn to something in the other lord's hand. "What have you got there, Monteagle?"

"We're not quite sure, old boy," said Monteagle, handing Sir Robert a piece of paper. "But we thought you ought to take a look at it."

Sir Robert carefully unfolded the paper and read the note out loud: *"Everyone who loves not the king should stay away from the Palace of Westminster and our hell-fire on November 5th."*

"Where did you get this?" asked Sir Robert.

"Someone put it through my door late last night," said Monteagle.

"It's very strange," said Suffolk. "What in heaven's name is 'hell-fire'?"

Jack suddenly felt a chill run down his spine.

"Do you think that might mean gunpowder?" he said. "I've heard it described that way before."

"Brilliant, Jack!" said Sir Robert. "I'm sure you're right. This must be from the plotters – it seems they mean to blow up Parliament today."

"Why would they send it to me?" said Lord Monteagle. "I'm a king's man."

"I believe you," said Sir Robert. "They made a mistake, but that's good for us. We need to search the entire building. Call the guards, Jack!"

"Right away, sir," said Jack, and he ran off to do his master's bidding.

"My lords Monteagle and Suffolk — would you be so good as to take some men and search the cellars?" asked Sir Robert. "There isn't a moment to lose!"

CHAPTER FiVE

"Remind me why we're down here again?" muttered Monteagle. He brushed dirt and dust from his expensive jacket with a lace handkerchief.

"Not sure I really know, old chap," said Suffolk, peering into the darkness.

The two lords were leading a squad of guards on a search of the cellars below Parliament. So far, they had found nothing but rats.

"Wait a moment," Monteagle. "I think I can hear something."

The guards raised their weapons. Suddenly, Fawkes and Keyes appeared out of the gloom. They were clearly surprised to see Monteagle and Suffolk and the guards.

"Halt, I say!" yelled Suffolk. "Just who the devil are you two men?"

"I'm John," said Fawkes, thinking fast. "John Johnson."

"What are you doing down here?" said Suffolk.

"We've been helping to organise the stores," said Keyes, quickly.

"Yes, piling up barrels," confirmed Fawkes.

"Oh yes, lots of barrels," said Keyes, and he sniggered. Fawkes glared at him.

"Have either of you men seen anyone or anything suspicious?" asked Suffolk.

"No, sir," said Fawkes. "Nothing at all."

"Well, that's good," said Monteagle, nodding. "On your way, then. And if you do see anyone suspicious, make sure you report them, all right?"

"We will, sir," said Fawkes. "You can trust us."

Fawkes and Keyes walked off, trying not to hurry away too obviously. Suffolk and Monteagle turned and continued with their search. After a while, they bumped into Sir Robert and Jack, who had also come down to the cellars.

"Well, my lords," said Sir Robert. "Have you found anything?"

"We've drawn a complete blank," said Suffolk.

"But we did meet a couple of nice chaps," said Monteagle. "Although, come to think of it they shouldn't have been down here, should they?"

"Which way did they go?" cried Sir Robert.

Both lords pointed and Sir Robert led the guards in that direction. Jack desperately hoped that it wasn't too late!

CHAPTER SIX

Fawkes and Keyes had just added the last barrel of gunpowder to the stack. Fawkes picked up a smaller barrel and pulled out the stopper. Then, he walked backwards from the stack, slowly pouring a thin trail of gunpowder on to the cellar floor.

"Right, are you ready?" he said when the barrel was empty. "All we have to do is light the fuse and get out of here."

"Of course I'm ready," said Keyes. "But are you sure the fuse is long enough? That amount of gunpowder will blow this whole building sky high."

"We should have a couple of minutes to make our escape," said Fawkes, patting his pockets. "I seem to have forgotten my flint."

"I've brought mine," said Keyes. Fawkes held out his hand, but Keyes shook his head. "Please let me light the fuse, Guy. I love doing that!"

"Oh, go on then," said Fawkes, with a sigh. "Just hurry up, will you?"

Keyes knelt by the powder fuse. He struck his flint once, then again, but failed to make a spark. He tried a third time and a spark leapt from the stone to the powder, which started to hiss and splutter. A small flame began to move along it, heading steadily towards the stack of barrels.

Just then, Sir Robert and Jack came round the corner, followed by the guards and Monteagle and Suffolk. Fawkes and Keyes looked round, surprised to have been caught.

"Stop, you villains!" yelled Sir Robert. "Seize those two men, guards!"

The guards rushed forward but Fawkes and Keyes were soldiers themselves, so they drew their swords and prepared to fight back. Steel clashed on steel in the gloomy cellar, and Fawkes and Keyes roared their defiance.

"You'll never take us alive!" cried Fawkes. "You're all going to die, too!"

"Not if I can help it!" yelled Jack, who had seen the sparks by the stack of barrels. He rushed over to the fuse and stamped it out with seconds to spare before it reached the first barrel.

"Well done, Jack!" said Sir Robert, clapping him on the back.

The struggle went on for a few more minutes, but Fawkes and Keyes were outnumbered.

Eventually, the guards overwhelmed them, knocking the men's swords from their hands and forcing the plotters down on to their knees.

"I'll bet you're not the only men involved in this plot," said Cecil, looking down on them. "I want the names of the other plotters."

"Down with the king!" cried Fawkes. "You'll get no names from me."

"Nor from me," growled Keyes. "Mr Catesby wouldn't like us to tell you his name. Er… whoops! Perhaps I shouldn't have said that."

"You fool, Keyes!" shouted Fawkes. "Don't say another word!"

"He doesn't need to," said Sir Robert, smiling. "We'll track down Catesby, and he'll soon lead us to the others. Take them away, men."

The guards dragged the men off. Jack watched them go.

"What will happen to them, sir?" he asked.

"Nothing very pleasant," Cecil answered. "They will be tortured and then hung, drawn and quartered. After they've been put on trial, of course."

Sir Robert and Jack made their way back to the king. He was waiting impatiently for them outside the Parliament's main chamber. Jack could hear a buzz of expectation beyond the doors.

"What in heaven's name has been going on, Sir Robert?" the king asked nervously. "Who were those wretched men I saw being taken away?"

"A couple of villains who were plotting against you, Your Majesty," said Sir Robert. "But I am proud to say that we caught them just in time."

"Jolly good," said the king. "I'm just about to make my opening speech,"

"We wouldn't miss it for the world," said Sir Robert.

He rolled his eyes at Jack as they followed the king into the main chamber. They had saved the day!

GLOSSARY

Catholic
someone who believes the Pope is the head of their religion

execute
to carry out a death sentence

fuse
a length of material along which a flame moves to explode gunpowder

gunpowder
a type of explosive

Protestant
someone who believes that the king or queen is head of the Church of England

torture
to cause someone a lot of pain